Icefall

by

John Townsend

Illustrated by Pulsar Studios

You do not need to read this page –
just get on with the book!

First published in 2009 in Great Britain by
Barrington Stoke Ltd
18 Walker St, Edinburgh, EH3 7LP

www.barringtonstoke.co.uk

ISBN: 978-1-84299-570-9

Printed in Great Britain by Bell & Bain Ltd

AUTHOR ID

Name: John Townsend

Likes: Skiing down a snowy mountain without falling over.

Dislikes: Falling over! Losing my skis, spinning down the slope and ending up head-first in a snow-drift.

3 words that best describe me:
A great skier (some hopes!)

A secret not many people know: I was once questioned by armed Austrian police in my Mickey Mouse pyjamas because our school ski party was suspected of robbing the hotel safe!

ILLUSTRATOR ID

Name: Ian from Pulsar Studios

Likes: Drawing, music and lasagne.

Dislikes: Getting up very very early.

3 words that best describe me:
Humour, determination and utopia.

A secret not many people know:
My dad wanted me to be a football goalkeeper.

To the boys of Rhondda-Cynon-Taf Libraries "Read a Million Words Together in Wales" project.

Contents

Intro

If you read *Deadline*, you'll know about Barney.

He's in the news because he and his friend, Laura, stopped a terrorist from blowing up a plane at the airport. The papers are full of it. He and Laura were on a school skiing trip. Now they can't catch the same plane as the rest of their class. They have to wait and talk to the police about what happened.

At last the fuss dies down and they can fly off to Austria. They join their friends. The week ahead's going to be so cool. All they want is to chill and enjoy the mountains. How wrong they are!

Danger's never far away when Barney's around ...

Chapter 1
A Face at the Window

It was the noise that woke him. Not a loud noise, but a soft creak. Just outside the window.

Barney opened his eyes but the hotel room was dark. Solid black. All he could see was a red **01:21** on the bedside clock. He sat up. His heart was racing. As he slid out of bed, he heard a sound at the window. From the balcony. His room was four floors up.

He didn't put on the light. He felt his way round the bed and crept towards the window. The curtains were shut but Barney could see a light flickering outside. A torch.

He shivered. He reached out to touch the curtain. As he slowly pulled it back, he froze. A dark shape moved on the balcony outside, crunching on ice. Barney wiped the glass and peered out into the snowy night. It was then he saw a face. A mean face with cruel eyes. And a silver nose-stud.

Barney dropped to the floor. Had the eyes seen him? He crouched behind the curtain and waited in the darkness. Now he wished he had a friend with him in the room. There was no one to talk to here. Mrs Peters had given him a room of his own because of all the drama on the way over. His friend Laura had her own room too. She was only across the corridor but Barney felt very alone as he hid in the dark. He didn't know what to do.

Just what was the man doing outside his window? And who was with him?

Holding his breath, Barney waited and listened. There were two voices outside. Barney slowly stood up. He couldn't make out what they were saying but it sounded as if they were talking in English. Maybe it was safe to take another look. Once more he touched the curtain and peeped out. The man was kneeling on the balcony with a bag of tools. A woman stooped beside him. In the murky moonlight, all Barney could see was the back of her head. Her hair was short and her neck had a dark mark on it. The torch flashed over it and Barney saw it was a tattoo of a snake.

Barney groped around in the darkness. His hand found a ski-pole. It wasn't much of a weapon but at least he could lash out with it if they attacked. He gripped it firmly and stepped towards the balcony door. His other hand touched the handle. It was time to act. He turned the lock and pushed the door. But he wasn't ready for what happened next. He blinked as icy wind stung his eyes. As he rubbed them and peered into the darkness, he couldn't believe what he saw. Nothing. No one was there. The balcony was empty. There were just footprints in a dusting of snow. Footprints with zigzags across them.

Barney stepped slowly out on the ice in his bare feet. He gasped – it was so cold. He tip-toed over to the rail to look down to the street below. It was dark down there. The dim light from a street lamp seeped through swirling snow. Tiny flakes danced in the cold wind … as two shadows sped into a door-way. Barney should have been thrilled to see the fresh snow falling – great for skiing in the morning. But now it didn't matter. Something odd was going on. He leaned over to get a better look at where the shadows had gone. That was when he heard the crack … as the balcony rails broke around him and he lurched forward. His ski-pole dropped from his hand, spinning down to the snowy street far below. His feet slipped off the edge ... and he fell out into the night.

Chapter 2
Falling from Ice

For a split second Barney felt like he was flying. Like one of his big jumps at the gym. But now he wasn't sailing through the air from a spring-board on the gym floor. This was serious falling. Many times he'd taken a tumble from the ropes or bars when his body seemed to hang in mid-air. Like in slow-motion – as his brain tried to catch up. Now his mind was in a mad spin. How could he get out of a nose-dive to the street below? His body turned and twisted as he stretched his arms to catch hold of something. He'd won cups and shields for his gym skills but no contest had been like this. There were no crash-mats here. This wasn't the gym. This was for real.

The freezing air rushed past his ears. He sucked in and felt it stab his lungs. His eyes watered and his heart seemed to burst in his chest. As he fell past the window below, he saw the rope. It hung from the corner of his balcony. It was his only hope. It rushed past him as his body dropped like a stone.

Twisting his hips and diving sideways, Barney grabbed at the rope. He held onto it with both hands, almost tugging his arms from their sockets. He gripped it hard with freezing fingers. As he swung out over the street, he spun round and crashed back into the rails of the balcony below. But he clung on and gripped the rope between his knees. He wouldn't have won any prizes for style,

but he'd saved himself from crashing to the street. With a sigh of relief, he began to climb up the rope. His bare feet pushed him up bit by bit. The snowy wind cut right through him. At last his numb fingers pulled him up to the edge of his balcony. The rope stretched right down to the ground below. To footprints in the snow. With zigzags.

Barney swung his legs onto the balcony and pulled himself up. He slipped on the ice and almost took another dive. But he grabbed the balcony door. He shivered and his hands shook as he looked down to the street where the broken railings lay twisted in the snow. To where he'd nearly smashed into the ground. To where footprints led across the snow into a dark doorway. To where a figure stood in the shadows ... looking up at him. Staring up in the moonlight.

Chapter 3
The Finger of Blame

It was almost two o'clock in the morning. Barney sat on the bed in his ski jacket and jeans. It took a long time for him to stop shivering and feel warm again. His mind was still in a spin. Who had been out there on the balcony and why? What was going on?

There was no way Barney could get back into bed and forget about what had just happened. But he wasn't sure what to do. In fact, now he thought about it, since he'd arrived in Austria two days ago, he'd felt odd. As if someone was watching him.

Suddenly he heard a creak in the corridor. He ran to listen at the keyhole but he didn't dare open the door. Or was he imagining things? He stood up with a sigh. This was mad. He needed to talk to someone. He'd go and wake Laura.

Barney crept along the corridor, looking round every time he heard the smallest sound. A dim light at the far end cast creepy shadows across the wall. He waited outside Laura's room. He had to talk to her. She'd help him think straight. He needed to tell her that two people had just tried to kill him by sawing through the rails on his balcony.

Barney raised his hand to knock on Laura's door. Just before the first knock, he froze. He heard a noise somewhere behind him. He turned to peer down the gloomy corridor. Nothing. But he was sure someone had been watching him. He crept to the main stairway where a strip-light buzzed over the stairs. A door slammed. The sound of running feet drifted up the stairs. He crept slowly down to the floor below ... and then to the next. He heard distant voices. They were coming from the hall-way below. He peered over the stair rail. But he didn't lean on it – not this time.

The bottom step and the hallway beyond were in a pool of orange light. Barney crept down further, straining to listen to the voices. There were two. Soft and in English. Male and female. He couldn't hear what they were saying. The bottom step creaked under his foot. He ran into the shadows to hide by a cupboard. One of the voices spoke.

"Did you hear something?" It was a man's voice, with a German accent.

Barney heard footsteps coming towards him on the wooden floor. A girl's voice close by whispered, "I can't see anything."

He knew that voice. He gave a sigh and stepped out from where he was hiding.

"Laura, what are you doing here?" he asked.

Laura gasped. "Barney, it's you! You really scared me. Can't you sleep either?"

He looked past her into the gloom. "I heard noises and ... who's that with you?"

"It's Hans – the ski instructor. Come and join us. We're at the table having a chat and hot chocolate."

Hans was just behind Laura. He was very tall, with spiky tinted hair that made him look even taller. "Hi, Barney. What are you doing out of bed? You're my star pupil! You need your sleep for another hard day on the slopes. The fresh snow will be great ..."

"I don't care right now, Hans. I'm scared," Barney said softly.

Laura held Barney's arm. "What's up, Barney? You look a bit pale."

Barney sat at the table and put his head in his hands. "I know this sounds kind of weird, but someone was on my balcony and I think they tried to kill me."

"Barney, all that stuff is over now. Relax. Chill." Laura laughed. "You may not know this, Hans, but Barney's a bit of a star back home. He's been in all the papers and on the news. You see, he heard two men planning to blow up a plane. We stopped them just in time."

"Wow!" Hans said. "A hero, eh? With big ideas to save the world."

"Please listen." Barney thumped the table. "This is real. I fell off my balcony. They cut the rails. I almost got killed. I grabbed the rope just in time and ..."

"Woo! This is all a bit James Bond." Hans grinned. "I guess you were having a dream, yes?"

Barney kicked the table hard. "I mean it. I'm not making it up. You believe me, don't you, Laura?"

"Er ... yeh. Sure. Anything you say, Barney. Anyone for more hot chocolate?"

Barney stood up and kicked his chair over. He was shouting now. "You don't believe me. Would I make it up? Someone was on my balcony, I tell you. When I went out there they'd gone. But they'd sawn through the rails. They broke when I went out and I fell. There was a rope. That's how they got away.

I saw them down in the street. In the snow. They tried to kill me."

Hans waved his hand. "OK. OK. Cool it. Calm down. You've had a long day. You're tired. We all are."

Barney walked back to the stairs. "I'm not staying here to be called a liar." He swore. "If I didn't go to gym club, I'd be dead by now. I had to use all my gym skills so as not to crash into the ground. Maybe you'd believe me then – *when I'm dead*. When it's too late."

Laura ran over to him. "Sorry, Barney. But why on earth would anyone want to kill you? After all, you're so cute!" She stroked his chin. "With such sad puppy-eyes ..."

He didn't smile. "I can show you. Right now. Come up and take a look."

Hans began to climb the stairs. "Yeh, you do that. Take us to the scene of the crime, Mister Bond ..."

As soon as they were in Barney's room, he ran to the window. The rails on the balcony were still missing.

"Look, the rails have gone and if you look down you'll see their footprints and the rope ..." Barney stood still and stared.

"What's up, Barney?" Laura peered down to the street.

He was stunned. "It's not there. The rope's gone. And fresh snow's covered the prints."

Hans said nothing but his look said it all.

"I didn't dream it," Barney shouted.

"Nor did I," someone said behind them. Mrs Peters stood in the doorway. She looked very angry.

"I do not expect to be woken by the manager of this hotel in the middle of the night, Barney Jones. He tells me someone reported you shouting abuse from the balcony and sounding very drunk. That isn't very clever for a 13-year-old, is it?"

"That's just not true, Mrs Peters. Honest," Barney said.

She stormed past him and reached down by the bed. "In that case, young man, you'd better explain this to me." She picked up a half-empty bottle and sniffed it.

"How dare you have this in your room. It's vodka."

Chapter 4
Trouble

At breakfast Mrs Peters gave Barney one of her icy looks. She got up and came over to where Barney and Laura were sitting.

"Just wait till I tell your father about last night, young man. When he hears you broke my 'NO DRINK' rule, I'm sure he'll have a lot to say," she began.

"Yes, he will," Barney sulked. "When I tell him *my* side of the story."

"And that's all it is, Barney. A story," Mrs Peters went on. "You made it up. Your father knows you only too well. You like to be in the spot-light. You always have to be noticed. You do anything to show off. Well, this time you've gone too far. I've a good mind to call your father right now. Don't you dare give me any more trouble today." She glared at him, then stormed off.

"Don't worry about her," Laura said. "She'll get over it."

"But I won't," Barney said. "It's not just that no one believes me. I'm used to that. It's that someone is out to get me. They hid that vodka in my room. And now I think about it, there was something in my drink of coke last night. It tasted odd. I couldn't drink it. I just thought that's what coke tastes like over here. Now I'm sure it was drugged. This is scary, Laura. But it's no use telling her ..."

He looked over to where Mrs Peters had been sitting. "I hate her."

Laura patted his head. "Cheer up. Look outside. It's sunny and there's great snow."

The ski slopes were superb. As soon as Hans took his group through the woods, Barney put his worries to the back of his mind. He was too busy trying to dodge in and out of the trees. Hans sped ahead and stopped at the top of a steep slope. Barney swept to a halt behind him, spraying him with powder snow. They all cheered before getting into a snowball fight. Soon everyone was covered in snow and laughing. Hans pointed across the valley to a huge cliff of ice that glinted in the sun. It looked like a painting. There was a tiny chalet perched on purple rock jutting above the blue-tinted ice.

"That icefall is called Death Leap. People get killed there every year. No one survives a fall over that waterfall of ice. Don't worry, Barney, we won't jump off it today!" Hans laughed.

Barney smiled. "If you go off that, it'll be 'Look, no Hans!'" Everyone groaned and pelted Barney with snowballs.

Later on Hans took Barney snow-boarding on his own. The rest of the party went sight-seeing in the town.

Mrs Peters had made a point of telling everyone, "I'll only take those of you I can trust. Barney will stay with Hans."

"You're doing very well, Barney," Hans shouted from the top of a bank of snow. "Try a jump off here like this ..." He leapt in the air and landed with a bow. Barney sped over and did exactly the same.

"Perfect, Barney. Well done. You're a great ski student. You even impress the

locals. That man took some photos of you snow-boarding so well."

"What man?" Barney looked round. There was no one there.

"He was there just now. Someone out for a walk. Big camera. Zoom lens."

Barney looked scared. "What did he look like?"

"I didn't take much notice," Hans said. "He had a rucksack and stick."

"What about his face?"

"No idea. Dark glasses ... head band ... oh yes, and a nose stud."

There was a little café up on the top ski slopes. Hans said they'd done enough snow-boarding and should take a break there.

Sitting in the warm café Barney stirred his hot chocolate and spoke softly. "The thing is, Hans, that nose-stud guy is after me. It's creepy. Nose-stud *and* Tattoo Woman. They were the ones on my balcony. It's like I'm being watched all the time."

"Don't worry," Hans said firmly, "I'll stop anyone attacking you! Come on, I'll treat you to a big cake. That'll cheer you up." Hans clumped over to the counter in his ski boots. A band began to play in the corner and a woman came over and sat at Barney's table. She said something in German so Barney just nodded. He stared at her. He didn't feel he could trust anyone any more. Was she safe or was she about to drop poison in his drink? He turned to see where Hans was. But no one was there. Hans had gone.

Barney ran outside. Hans's snow-board had gone too. Where was he? Surely he wouldn't go without saying anything. "You can't trust anyone round here," Barney muttered. He picked up his own snow-board and walked across the snow. Maybe Hans was still around somewhere. Barney looked across the mountain for Hans's bright red ski hat. It was then he saw him getting on the chair-lift. Barney ran and got on a chair behind the red hat. As soon as he sat down, Barney shouted and waved. The person in the red hat turned and waved. It wasn't Hans at all.

Just then a shot ripped through the empty chair next to Barney. A hole tore through the back of the seat just centimetres from his back. He turned to look over his shoulder at the chair behind his. A man in a hood was aiming what looked like a ski pole right at him. Suddenly another shot tore into the back of the seat, even closer this time. Barney was a sitting target and he knew it. The next shot could be the last he heard. There was nothing for it. Barney had to get off fast – and jump.

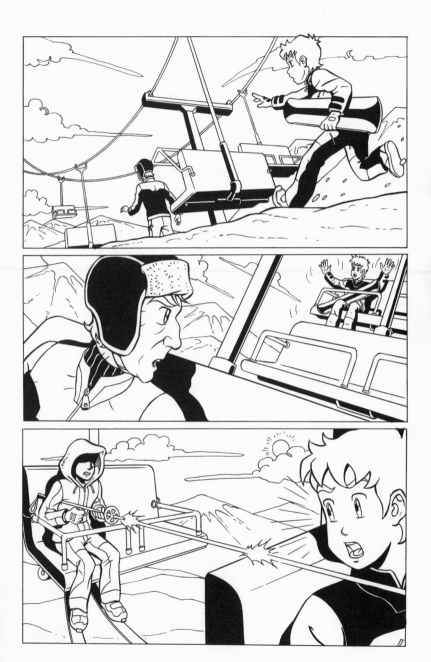

The chair-lift rose above the top of trees. It was now or never. Without stopping to think twice, Barney threw his snow-board into the trees and slid from his seat. He grabbed the foot-rail and hung below the chair ... just as another shot hit where he'd been sitting. His feet brushed the top of trees, still thick with snow. As the chair-lift passed over the top of the next tree, Barney let go. He tried to tell himself it was just another jump from the bars at the gym as he fell through the branches. They cracked and flicked his face, showering him with snow which stung his eyes. He crashed through the trees, snapping twigs as he fell. Half-way down, he hit a large branch that tore his shin. That hurt! He grabbed the branch and swung to catch another further down before dropping into a snow drift. He landed in a heap. He was winded and his gloves were ripped so his fingers were bleeding. But he was still in one piece.

The snow was deep. It was hard to push his way through but at last Barney found his snowboard. Then he sped off down the mountain. He wasn't sure how many shots he heard behind him. But he was soon beyond range as he raced down the valley. On to get help. Yet who was going to believe him now?

Chapter 5
Missing

"I tell you, Laura, they shot at me. I can't prove it but they did." Barney sat on her bed with his head in his hands.

"I believe you Barney," Laura told him. "I didn't before. Sorry. I thought you were just mucking about. But I can see by your face it's true. You look really scared."

"I am. But at least you know now. The more I think about Hans, the more worried

I am. Where did he go? He'd never go off without saying anything. I tried to tell Mrs Peters but she said, 'Of course he left you. You're just a silly little boy. He got fed up with you. So don't make a fuss. Hans knows the slopes like the back of his hand so you don't have to make a drama out of this. He just went home, that's all.'"

Laura couldn't help giggling. Barney had said all that in a Mrs Peters' voice and he did it so well. But Barney wasn't laughing.

"The thing is, Laura, it's not a joke. I've never been this scared."

"I know, Barney. I can tell. I want to help you."

"I think Hans must be in danger. If someone's after me, Hans is in the way. If they get rid of him, they can then get me. I've got to go back and look for him. The last time I saw him was up in that café on the slopes. I need to get back up there before it closes."

Laura looked at her watch. "Then we'd better hurry. It shuts in half an hour. It'll be dark soon. I'll come with you. I'll take my mobile. We'll have to sneak out without Mrs Peters seeing us."

By the time they reached the café, the sun was sinking behind the mountains. Most people had left the slopes and the café was empty apart from a man sweeping the floor.

"Do you speak English?" Laura asked him.

"Try me," he said.

Barney spoke slowly and loud. "Have you seen a man here? My ski teacher, Hans. He wears a red hat and ..."

"Sure. I know Hans," the man said. "He was here today. He got ill. They take him up the mountain. Over that valley to the chalet. He need sleep. I think he drink too much." The man tapped his nose and laughed.

"How do we get there?" Laura asked.

The man pointed. "Chair-lift. But you must hurry. It close soon."

Barney looked at his watch. "Tell me," he said. "Who took Hans?"

"Man in black glasses. With stud in nose."

Barney and Laura ran out into the snow. "We've got to get up to that chalet," Barney said. They ran to the chair-lift.

"How will we get down again?" Laura asked. "It'll be dark and all the lifts will be shut. I think we should call Mrs Peters. Just so she knows. She'll go mad but ..." She tapped the number on her mobile and swore. "It's no good. There's no signal here."

Barney thought hard. "If Nose Stud is up there, we should get the police. He's evil. Can you run back to the café and use their phone? I'll go ahead on my own. We can't waste time."

"Take care, Barney," Laura called as she ran back to the café. "Don't do anything daft ..."

"No, Mrs Peters!" he yelled, as he got on the chair-lift.

"You can't go up on your own," the chair-lift man said. "Kids must go with an adult."

Barney gave a sigh. "It's important. I've got to get up the mountain fast. I've lost someone."

"Not on your own." The man pressed the button to stop the lift. Barney wanted to scream.

"It's OK. I'll go with him," a woman holding skis said. "If that helps."

"Thanks," Barney said with relief. "That's great. Thanks a lot."

They both sat down and the chair-lift swung out over the snow and rose above the trees.

"You're not going snow-boarding on your own I hope," the woman said. "Not just you and a snow-board."

"No. I need to get to the chalet up the mountain across the valley."

"The chalet above the icefall? Rather you than me. It'll be dark and freezing by the time you get there."

"Yeh, I know. It's already a bit nippy," Barney said. He rubbed his hands together.

"I've got some hot coffee in my flask if you'd like some," the woman said. She began to pour some into a cup.

"Thanks," Barney said. "I can do with it if I've got to cross the mountain to that chalet."

He took a sip. It tasted odd, like the coke last night. He looked up, not sure what to say. The woman was putting the flask back in her ruck-sack when Barney saw her neck. With a tattoo of a snake.

"Drink it all up," she said. "I won't want it."

"I bet you won't," Barney gasped. "I bet you gave most of it to Hans. You're not going to get rid of me that easily ..." He threw away the cup.

"Then you'll have to take the poison this way," she shouted. She stabbed at him with a syringe. The needle stuck into his shin.

Barney stared at her with a groan, then slumped over the safety bar of the chair-lift with a groan. Tattoo Woman leaned over him to pull him off the bar. She lifted the bar up so as to push Barney out of the chair. She kicked his feet off the foot-rail and pushed. That's when Barney grabbed her arm and pulled her past him. She slid from her seat and screamed as she fell off the chair-lift. She tried to grab his legs but he moved them away fast and she dropped ... falling onto the rocks far below. She hit them with a thud and her screams stopped.

Barney sat dazed. He pulled the safety bar back. Then he reached down and pulled the needle out of his shin-pad. Now he was glad he'd hurt his shin when he'd jumped off the chair-lift before. Because of that he'd put on the extra shin-pad when he and Laura went out again. He wrapped the syringe in a blob of tissue and then looked down to where the woman lay in the snow with her neck bent and twisted. He was shocked. He hadn't meant to hurt her but why had she tried to kill him? He looked across at the chalet. Maybe he'd find the answer there. It would take him a while to reach it. He hoped the police were on their way. Laura should have got hold of them by now.

But Laura hadn't phoned the police yet. She hadn't been able to. She was tied up in the cellar of the café.

Chapter 6
The Chalet

Barney looked in the chalet window. It was dark inside. He knocked on the door. Nothing. It was locked. Maybe there was nothing here at all. He looked at all the footprints in the snow. Footprints with zigzags on the soles. Now he knew he had to get inside.

An upstairs window was just open so Barney was soon clambering up the wall. With shutters and wooden slats to give him foot-holds, climbing was easy. Very soon he was on the window sill, lifting the window and climbing inside. The room was empty so he crept on to a landing and down wooden stairs. He heard heavy breathing from behind one of the doors. His hand touched the handle and the door creaked open.

The room was dark, the shutters closed. Barney switched on a light and there, slumped on a wooden chair, was Hans. He was asleep, tied up, with tape over his mouth.

"Hans, it's me. Wake up." Barney shook him and peeled off the tape. Hans was dazed. He blinked at Barney for a long time.

"Barney?" he groaned. "Ah, my head. They drugged me. Where is the man?"

"It's OK," Barney whispered. "No one's here. I'm going to get you help. The police are on their way ..."

"Wrong!" A booming voice filled the room as a man barged in and kicked Barney to the floor. A man with mean eyes – and a nose stud. "You're wrong about no one being here. You're wrong about the police. But you, kid, you took the bait. Just as I planned. I knew you'd come to find your friend. I followed you up the mountain and saw you climb in the window. I've been looking forward to this ..."

He hit Barney in the face, grabbed his throat and dragged him to a chair. Despite his struggles, Barney was soon tied up with thick ropes on the chair..

"I won't tape your mouth," Nose Stud gave a nasty grin. "You can scream as much as you like. There's no one for miles. In fact, I'll enjoy hearing you squeal. You're going to suffer before you die."

"What have I done? Why do you want to kill me?" Barney stared at Nose Stud as if the answer was on his face.

"Because I hate you," Nose Stud snarled. "You get in the way. You talk too much. So I've got to get rid of you ..." He took a large can from the corner and poured petrol on the floor.

"This place will go up in minutes. There'll be nothing left. A few of your bones, maybe. You can forget about the police getting here. I tied up your friend in the café. Unlucky."

He kicked Barney's shin. It hurt. "That's for what you did to my friend. I saw her dead on the rocks. Another reason to kill you."

He picked up a bottle. More petrol. He splashed it over Barney's lap and then smashed the bottle on the chair.

"That will make sure you cook well. There's no way you'll be going to the trial now."

"The trial?" Barney didn't understand what Nose Stud meant.

"My brother's trial, you fool," Nose Stud growled. "It was you who got my brother arrested. He was the guy at the airport hotel. Your girlfriend tied him up in the hotel room and the police got him. They want you to tell your story in court and then they can put him away for years. But not now ... Now I've got you and you can't give your evidence. Your side of the story's soon going to be lost forever."

"You're mad!" Barney shouted. "You won't get away with this."

"That's just where you're wrong." Nose Stud struck a match and threw it. A sheet of flame shot across the floor with a roar. "Have a nice fry-up!" he laughed as he ran from the room. Fire ripped up the walls and the room filled with black smoke.

Barney wriggled in his chair. He held his breath. He was not going to scream. The rope was tight round his arms but he could move his fingers. They touched something sharp that was stuck in the back of his chair. Broken glass from the smashed bottle. It was just within reach. Barney gripped the glass and rubbed its sharp edge against the rope round his waist. The smoke and heat were choking him and his fingers bled but he didn't care. The room was ablaze. If a spark fell on him, he knew he'd burst into a fire-ball.

As the glass cut the rope, Barney broke free and fell on the floor. There wasn't time to untie Hans. He'd passed out. Barney grabbed his chair and dragged him to the door. As he opened it, a blast of air fanned

the flames and the whole room burst into a raging blaze. Barney threw himself out of the front door, pulling Hans with him. It was hard to lift Hans' lifeless body as they both fell into the snow. The chalet behind them exploded in a roar of flames. The mountain around them lit up as red smoke rolled into the sky.

Suddenly Nose Stud was there again – beside them, on skis. He waved an ice-axe above his head and aimed it at Barney. It smashed down by his ear. Barney rolled away, grabbed Nose Stud's ski and pulled him to the ground. They rolled through the snow ... crashing down a slope. Arms, legs, skis and the ice-axe flew across the ice. Behind them the sky flashed with fire.

Nose Stud threw himself onto Barney and held him by the throat. "I'll have to strangle you instead," he hissed. His thumbs dug into Barney's neck. Barney couldn't move or breathe with the man on his chest. All he could do was reach into his belt-bag. He fumbled inside and pulled out the syringe. He lifted it up, just as Nose Stud pressed his knee into Barney's throat. Barney slammed the needle into the man's leg. Nose Stud screamed. He kicked Barney down a rocky drop. Barney spun down across the ice, just grabbing the ice-axe as he hurtled towards a sheer drop – the terrible icefall – Death Leap.

Barney hacked the ice-axe into a crack in the ice cliff and it held. He clung on, as his legs swung out over the cliff. He tried to clamber up but his feet slipped off the ice. He could only cling on for dear life ... as Nose Stud looked down at him in a rage.

When Barney looked up again, Nose Stud's feet were at his fingers. He was about to kick the ice-axe over the edge. The needle still stuck into his leg as he stumbled around.

He swayed and swore – and seemed to be drunk. Barney held on tight.

"Get ready for a long drop," Nose Stud groaned. The drug was making him sleepy. Before he could kick the ice-axe away, he slumped forward. He groaned as he fell. He slid across the ice and spun off the cliff. His scream filled the valley below and died away – as he fell silently into the icy darkness.

Barney couldn't hold on any more. The ice-axe was slipping. He cried in horror. He was going to die after all.

Suddenly a roar and a blazing light swept up the valley. A helicopter hung above him, just metres over the icefall. A rope dropped down and a man on the end of it looped Barney into a harness. They rose up into the helicopter and swept away across the mountain. Behind them flames still poured

from the chalet and smoke rolled angrily across the moon.

Chapter 7
The Ice Thaws

"Give me a bit of credit," Laura said. "Do you think I'd stay tied-up? My dad gave me a Swiss Army knife before I came skiing and it was in my ski jacket. Don't tell Mrs Peters! It didn't take me long to cut myself free and then I rang the police."

"It's just as well you did," Hans said. "Barney was seconds away from falling off Death Leap. I wouldn't have lasted long, either. Once the fire burnt out, I'd have frozen to death up there."

He ate another chip and sipped his coffee. "Thanks for all you did, Laura."

"Barney's the real hero. Not for the first time!" Laura said. She put down her fork. "This isn't bad for hospital food. How long do you think they'll keep us all here?"

"If we're OK, we'll be able to leave tomorrow. They just need to keep an eye on the three of us for the night. Then we'll have a day of police questions, I guess. Barney's been with them for over an hour already. Poor lad needs a break." Hans tried to stand up.

"Still a bit dizzy? Blame Mrs Peters. All her fussing made me go wobbly, too! I bet she's the one doing all the talking with Barney now. The police won't get a word in!"

Before Laura could finish, Barney walked in with a big grin.

"Guess what! They won't let us go home with the others on Saturday. The police need us to stay on next week. You'll have to look after us, Hans. Everything's paid for!"

Barney took a chip and laughed. "Mrs Peters is well mad!"

He didn't see that Mrs Peters was just behind him. She had followed him into the room.

"I have every reason to be mad, Barney. This is the last thing I wanted. You should never have gone off on your own like that. You know the ropes. Both of you."

"I think I've had enough of ropes," Barney said. Mrs Peters didn't smile. He got the icy glare. He tried to thaw it with a smile and one of his sad puppy-looks.

"Sorry, miss. Thanks for letting us stay on to sort things out with the police," he said.

"I have no choice," Mrs Peters snorted. "I just hope next time you come on a ski trip you won't try to act like James Bond all the time. It's all a bit much."

"Next time, Mrs Peters? You mean you'll let me come again?" Barney gave her his biggest smile.

"Of course," she said. "Why shouldn't I? You've done very well. You all have. Well done."

She walked from the room to talk to the doctor. Laura gave Barney a wink.

"You've melted her heart at last," she said.

"She still didn't say sorry for not believing me ..."

He stopped at the sudden sound of Mrs Peters shouting, **"I do not expect to be woken by the manager of this hotel in the middle of the night, Barney Jones."**

Hans was stunned. Laura looked round the room, her mouth open. Barney burst out laughing. "It's my mobile. What do you think of my new ring-tone? I recorded me doing her voice! Cool, eh?"

He took out his mobile. "Sorry," he turned back to Laura and Hans. "It's my mum."

"Hi. Yes, Mum," he went on, "Yes, Mum. Of course. Yes, Mum ..."

He put the phone back in his pocket. "My mum's flying out tomorrow. She says I'll need some more clean pants and a vest. So much for being a super-cool mega-hero! I bet James Bond never has this trouble ..."

"Maybe not," Laura winked. "But he always gets the girl in the end."

And she gave him a kiss ... like never before.

Barrington Stoke would like to thank all its readers for commenting on the manuscript before publication and in particular:

John Adamson
Chantelle Akelis
Beth Buchanan
Stephanie Carrick
Chris Chalmes
Stephanie Clark
Liam Conway
Fraser Courtney
Steven Dawkins
Davi Dmagee
Kenneth Fowley
Sarah Fraser
James Gillespie
Rhona Hamilton
Andrew Hepburn

Lauren Hunter
Lara Livingstone
Kayleigh MacKinnon
Jane MacMillan
Ryan McGowan
Christopher Mears
Kennedy Powell
Alun Powley
Callam Raesidle
Olivia Robson
Margaret Smith
Gary Stevely
Megan Sutherland
Jack Watson
Jordan Woods

Become a Consultant!

Would you like to give us feedback on our titles before they are published? Contact us at the email address below – we'd love to hear from you!

info@barringtonstoke.co.uk
www.barringtonstoke.co.uk